*Olga Takes Charge*

OTHER YEARLING BOOKS YOU WILL ENJOY:

YEARLING BOOKS are designed especially to entertain and enlighten young people. Charles F. Reasoner, Professor Emeritus of Children's Literature and Reading, New York University, is consultant to this series.

For a complete listing of all Yearling titles, write to Education Sales Department, Dell Publishing Co., Inc., 1 Dag Hammarskjold Plaza, New York, New York 10017.

# Olga Takes Charge

## MICHAEL BOND

### ILLUSTRATED BY HANS HELWEG

A YEARLING BOOK

Published by
Dell Publishing Co., Inc.
1 Dag Hammarskjold Plaza
New York, New York 10017

This work is published simultaneously in a hardcover volume entitled
*The Complete Adventures of Olga da Polga* by Delacorte Press, New York,
New York.

*Olga Takes Charge* was first published in Great Britain by Kestrel Books.

Text copyright © 1982 by Michael Bond

Illustrations copyright © 1982 by Hans Helweg

Yearling® TM 913705, Dell Publishing Co., Inc.

ISBN: 0-440-46620-2

Printed in the United States of America

First Yearling printing—April 1983

CW

# CONTENTS

CHAPTER ONE

# Olga Gives Advice

Graham was in love. There was no doubt about it. Olga first noticed it one spring morning when he came round the side of the house, crawled slowly past her hutch as if it didn't even exist, and then walked with unseeing eyes slap-bang into the closed door of Mr Sawdust's shed.

If it had been anyone else – Noel, the cat, or even Fangio, the hedgehog – they would have made a quick recovery and gone on their way. But in Graham's case, being a slow mover at the best of times, it took him some while to sort himself out. Having been knocked off course he moved on in the wrong direction and wasn't seen again until after lunch.

Having partaken of several succulent blades of grass, carefully folded in two from the middle so that she would get the most benefit from the least possible effort, Olga was about to retire to her bedroom for an afternoon nap when she heard a rustle in the near-by shrubbery.

This time she was better prepared. 'Watch out!' she squeaked, as Graham drew near. 'Wheeeeee! Wheeeeeeeeee!'

Graham paused and gazed up at her with a vacant expression on his face.

'Aren't you going to have your food?' asked Olga. 'Mrs Sawdust put some out for you specially.'

'Food!' Graham scoffed at the idea. 'That's all you guinea-pigs ever think about. There *are* other things in life, you know.'

Olga drew herself up. 'There won't be if you carry on like that,' she said. 'You won't *have* a life if you carry on like that. You'll be all shell and bones.'

8

Graham considered the matter for a moment. 'You're quite right,' he said. 'Quite right. I *must* keep up my strength.' And without further ado he moved towards the bowl which was standing outside the kitchen door.

Olga preened herself as a sound of steady lapping filled the air. She gave a sigh. There was no doubt about it. Guinea-pigs *knew* about things. It was something they were born with. How the other animals had managed before she came on the scene, goodness only knew. There was simply no one else to turn to for advice.

She waited for a while and then, during a pause in the lapping, posed the question which was uppermost in her mind.

'What's she like?'

Graham didn't answer for a moment or two. The fact of the matter was, although he wouldn't have admitted it to Olga, hunger had got the better of him and he had a large piece of bread stuck in his throat. Turning his head away, he pretended he was thinking hard. Olga, who thought he was choking with emotion, waited patiently.

'She's big,' admitted Graham at last, 'and ... er ... well, I suppose you'd just say ... she's big. Big for her size, that is ...'

Olga, her feminine instincts aroused, squeaked impatiently. 'There must be something else about her!' she exclaimed. 'How about her eyes?'

'They're big too,' said Graham. 'She's big all over.'

Olga took a deep breath. 'I mean ... what colour are they?'

Graham busied himself with the bowl of food again. Being in love made you hungry. 'I don't know,' he said at last.

'You don't know! *You don't know!*' Olga could hardly believe her ears. Tortoises! No wonder they had a reputation for being slow.

'You *must* have seen them,' she said.

For some reason or other Graham seemed to find the question slightly embarrassing. 'Well,' he said between mouthfuls. 'Yes, and then again ... no. I mean, I know they're there. They must be. But the thing is, well, she's big, you see, and they're a bit high off the ground.'

Olga gazed at Graham as he stood there looking up at her helplessly, a dribble of milk running down his chin. She didn't like to say anything, but she couldn't help feeling that if she'd been his new friend she might not have wanted to look at him either.

'There must be something else about her!' she exclaimed impatiently. 'What does she talk about? What does she say?'

'Well, er ...' Graham shifted uneasily under

Olga's piercing stare. 'She hasn't actually said anything . . . yet.

'But I know she'd like to,' he added hastily. 'It's just that she's very quietly spoken, and being so big her voice is a long way off the ground.'

Olga digested this latest piece of information. Happy though she was in her house with all its 'mod. cons.', as Karen Sawdust called them, there were times when she wished she could get out into the world and see things for herself. Apart from that, Graham's continual harping on the size of his new friend was beginning to irritate her.

'I once knew a giant guinea-pig,' she began, her imagination getting the better of her. 'The largest guinea-pig ever known in the whole world. He was so big I always knew when he was coming to see me because it got dark early. And he had wonderful fur. I mean . . . all guinea-pigs' fur is nice compared to other animals', like cats, for instance, but . . .'

Olga broke off. Graham had disappeared. Completely and utterly disappeared.

'Wheeeeeeee!' she squeaked in disgust, and

went into her bedroom in a fit of pique. If people wanted her advice about matters the least they could do was to stay and listen. Apart from that, she'd been rather enjoying building up to her story and she spent most of that afternoon busy with her day-dream, storing it up in her memory so that she could bring it out later when she had a better audience.

But gradually, as the day wore on, her thoughts returned more and more to Graham. He'd looked so forlorn as he'd blinked short-sightedly up at her. Something would have to be done about the matter.

Olga reached a decision. She went into her dining-room and gave voice to a loud squeak. The kind of squeak which she reserved for moments of great importance. Moments when she wanted to summon an audience.

'Graham's in love?' repeated Fangio. 'What does that mean?'

Olga sighed. Tortoises were bad enough, but hedgehogs! 'It's something you wouldn't know about on account of your prickles,' she said stiffly, 'but it can be very painful.'

She hesitated, wondering whether to try out

her new story, but thought better of it as Noel
came into view.

'What's up now?' he asked sleepily.

Olga told him about her earlier conversation
with Graham, embroidering it a little here and
there in order to make it as interesting as possible.

'If it's as big as all that,' said Noel hastily, '*I'm*
certainly not going down the garden to look for
it. It's bad enough having Karen Sawdust and

her friends playing war games, without being trampled on by a giant.'

For once Olga rather regretted her vivid imagination.

'Well, perhaps it's not as big as all that,' she admitted grudgingly. But Fangio and Noel had gone.

And then it happened. There was a pounding of feet and suddenly, without warning, a large, round shape loomed up in front of her. Olga gave a shriek of terror and scuttled into her bedroom as fast as her legs would carry her.

'There! I told you to be careful.' Karen Sawdust's voice reached Olga through the hay. 'Now you've frightened her. I expect she wondered what on earth it was.'

'It's only a tin hat,' said her friend defensively.

'It may be only a tin hat to you,' said Karen Sawdust severely, 'but to a guinea-pig it must look like a giant.'

There was another patter of feet, this time in the opposite direction, and then silence.

Olga stirred as the words sank in. 'Tin hat . . . giant . . .'

Suddenly she put two and two together. 'Tin hat . . . giant . . .' Graham had been in love with a tin hat all the time! No wonder he hadn't got anywhere. She couldn't wait to tell the others . . .

And then she paused, her romantic side taking over. Better to have loved a tin hat and lost than never to have loved at all.

Already an ending to her own story was taking shape. That's what she would do. She would tell Graham a story that would be so

good, so exciting, it would take his mind off the problem.

'Wheeee!' Olga gave a sigh of contentment as she snuggled down into her hay again. 'And it'll be so much better for him in the long run!'

CHAPTER TWO

# The Day the World Ran Dry

Olga really had intended thinking up a story for
Graham. As things turned out, something happened shortly afterwards which not only took
her mind off the matter, but while it lasted made
even Graham forget his troubles.

It all began when Mr Sawdust did something
called 'having a week off in order to take advantage of the fine weather'.

It all sounded very complicated to Olga, and
even when she overheard a conversation which
had to do with removing Venables, the toad,
from the garden pool and taking him to a

friend's house down the road, she didn't give it a great deal of thought.

The Sawdust family were always doing strange things and she had no doubt that she would find out all about their latest goings-on sooner or later. She'd long since learnt that if you spent most of your time in a hutch, life had a habit of coming to you in the end, provided, of course, that you were patient – and guinea-pigs were nothing if not patient. There wasn't much that went on in the neighbourhood that didn't get back to her in double quick time, either by way of Noel or via the various other inhabitants of the garden. She was quite content to wait.

Even when Mr Sawdust reappeared carrying a large plastic bucket containing the few gold-fish who normally shared the pool with Venables, she still wasn't over-bothered.

Olga had other, far more important things on her mind – like the state of her grass, for example. Olga liked her grass to be as moist as possible and normally she had no complaints whatsoever on the matter. The Sawdust family went to a great deal of trouble to make sure she always had an ample supply, and even during the winter they often went miles in their car in search of fresh supplies, making sure it was clean and not taken from ditches too near the road, where it tasted of oil and exhaust fumes. On the whole it was so good that Olga often went for days at a time without having to go near her water bowl, she got all the moisture she needed out of the succulent juices contained in the blades.

But it had been a very dry spring. All the Sawdust family agreed they could hardly remember when it had last rained, and with the lack of rain the grass had grown steadily drier and drier until, really, it was just like eating hay. Not that Olga minded hay, but hay was hay and grass was grass, and she liked a bit of both.

It got so bad that Olga could hardly picture what good grass tasted like. And then, just as the memory was on the tip of her mind, the banging started and drove it clean out again.

*Bang! Crash! Wallop! ... Bang! Bang! Crash! Crash! Wallop! Wallop!*

Olga was so startled she ran into her bedroom squeaking with fright. Burying her head deep

into the hay, she didn't come out again for the rest of the morning.

The hammering and banging went on until nearly lunchtime and it was followed in turn by the sound of digging and the scraping of a shovel against concrete. What it was Olga neither knew nor cared. All she knew was that the peace of her day had been disturbed.

The story she'd been about to make up for Graham had gone from her mind for ever and any thoughts she may have had about enjoying a quiet nap dreaming of things past was entirely out of the question.

It was late that same afternoon when Olga

woke to the sound of a faint scratching outside her hutch. It was followed by a series of snuffles and snorts. She pricked up her ears and blinked sleepily through her bedroom window.

It was Graham, in all probability returning from a wander in the garden, traces of which were clearly visible on his shell.

'Wheeeee!' she squeaked. Perhaps he would know what had been going on.

Olga hurried out to her dining-room and peered through the wire-netting door at the figure below. She was wide awake now and all agog for the latest news.

'She's gone,' said Graham briefly, as he caught sight of Olga. 'I've looked everywhere. In the bushes. Under the trees. In the strawberry patch. Behind the brussels sprouts. I can't even find any sort of a trail. It's a rum do and no mistake.'

22

Olga clucked impatiently. For a moment or two she was tempted to tell Graham the truth. Then she thought better of it. She knew Graham from old and in his present mood he was liable to go off again without so much as another word and probably wouldn't be seen again for days. In the nick of time she changed her clucking into a sort of a long-drawn-out sniff. Almost immediately she wished she hadn't, for there was a very strange smell coming from somewhere close at hand. She soon discovered why.

'I've even looked under the compost heap,' continued Graham. 'Just in case − you never know. Took me ages. I got lost and I couldn't find my way out again. Then I looked in the pool. I thought she might have fallen in. But that's empty.'

'Empty?' repeated Olga. 'The pool's *empty*? But it's *never* empty. It's never, ever been empty − not since the day it was made.'

And it was true. Olga could remember it all quite clearly. There had been a great deal of fuss at the time, especially when Mr Sawdust had turned the water on. Everyone had clapped and cheered as it spurted out of the ground at the top of the rockery, and had then run down through a series of small waterfalls into the main pool at the bottom. But all that had been a long time ago – several summers, in fact, until it was now so much a part of the garden that it had long since been taken for granted.

'Well, it's empty now,' said Graham briefly. 'Bone dry. There's a sort of hole in the bottom, but she couldn't have gone down that – it's much too small.' He gazed short-sightedly up at the sky. 'Perhaps she got carried off by a giant bird. That's why there's no trail. I've heard of giant birds,' he added darkly.

But Olga wasn't listening. Her mind was racing in all directions. Suddenly everything was falling into place. The way Mr Sawdust had been rushing around doing things. The removal of the occupants of the pond ... First Venables, then the goldfish. And now she came to think of it, she distinctly remembered a remark Mrs Sawdust had called through her kitchen door at the height of it all. 'Don't forget there's a water shortage,' she'd said.

Now she knew what had happened Mr Sawdust's reply seemed even more ominous. 'Don't worry', he'd said. 'I've managed to save most of it. I've pumped it into the old bath down the bottom of the garden.'

Olga felt a chill inside her stomach. Things must have reached a pretty pass if the Sawdust family were reduced to saving their water in an old bath. One of the things which made humans different from guinea-pigs was the way they treated water. They were forever washing things up in it, sitting in it, spraying themselves with it, and, – worst of all, pouring it all away afterwards.

She gave vent to a shrill squeak. 'Wheeeeeeeeee!' she shrieked, as she ran round

her dining-room. 'Wheeeeeeeeee! Help! Hellllp! The world's sprung a leak! The world's sprung a leak! Everything's run dry! Help! Hellllp!'

In her haste and excitement she very nearly knocked over her water bowl. Fortunately, it was wide, and had a flat bottom to stop any such thing happening. But it was a close shave, and, as she crouched down on the floor of the hutch waiting for some kind of reaction to her cries for help, she thanked her lucky stars that it had been no worse.

Noel was the first to arrive on the scene, not looking best pleased at having his afternoon nap disturbed. '*Now* what's going on?' he meeowed. 'It sounded as though you'd been trodden on. I was in the middle of a lovely dream about a nest of mice I'd found, too.'

'*Trodden* on?' repeated Olga. She opened her mouth in order to let Noel know exactly what she thought of such a suggestion, and then thought better of it as she caught sight of Fangio approaching slowly from the other direction. Fangio spent a lot of his time in an old box in the garage, so he was often late for meetings, but

Olga felt there was no point in wasting her breath until all her audience had assembled.

As soon as they were settled she repeated all that she'd heard from Graham, plus her own views as to what it meant, adding a little bit here and a little bit there as she went along, to make it all sound more interesting. Olga enjoyed telling a story and by the time she'd finished the others were in the hollow of her paw and hanging on her every word. Noel's jaw had dropped, Fangio's eyes were as large as saucers, and even Graham had quite forgotten about his lost love. It was all very satisfying.

'The thing is,' said Olga, 'what are we going to do about it?'

'*Do about it*?' The thought of doing something about the situation obviously hadn't occurred to the others. They gazed up at Olga in amazement.

'Serves them right if you ask me,' said Noel, glancing darkly towards the house. 'They're always wasting water. It might teach them a lesson. They'll just have to be like cats from now on – use their tongues for washing a bit more.'

Olga gave an impatient squeak. She felt

the others were missing the whole point of her story. 'You'll look a bit silly when your tongue's gone dry,' she said. 'It's rough enough as it is. Just you wait. When all the water's gone it'll be just like concrete.' Olga had once felt Noel's tongue on the end of her nose when he'd been exploring round her garden run, and she hadn't liked the feel of it at all.

'And what about the garden?' she continued. 'There won't be any lettuce leaves or insects. They'll all die and in the end we shall too. You can't live without water.'

The others digested this last remark.

'It's up to you all,' squeaked Olga, striking while the iron was still hot. 'It's up to you all to save the world.'

'It's up to *us*?' repeated Noel suspiciously. Somewhere along the line there seemed to have been a change of direction. 'I thought you said *we* must do something about it.'

'So we shall,' said Olga grandly. 'I shall be in charge and I shall think up a plan. I'd come and help out if I could, but I can't. You've no idea how helpless I feel, living in a hutch and not being able to *do* things.'

'It's no worse than being a tortoise and not being able to run fast,' said Graham.

'Or a cat that's put out in the snow when it doesn't want to go,' agreed Noel.

'Or being a hedgehog and have all your milk run away,' added Fangio.

Olga, who'd been about to defend her position, stopped in mid squeak.

'I don't see what losing your milk's got to do with it,' she said crossly.

'Well, you said all the water has disappeared out of the pond,' said Fangio patiently, 'so I expect it's got a crack in it.

'The same thing happened with my saucer of bread and milk the other evening. Mrs Sawdust put it outside the kitchen door as usual, and I'd just started to eat it as usual, and do you know, the saucer was cracked and all the milk started to run away. And do you know, when I pushed the bread against the crack with my nose, it stopped running away.'

It had been a long speech by Fangio's standards, so long he'd almost forgotten what he'd been going to say, so he paused for breath while he thought the matter over.

'Is that all?' demanded Olga, who was rather fed up at the way Fangio was getting all the attention.

'No, it isn't,' said Fangio firmly. 'Because when I ate the bread all the milk started to run out again.'

Noel was quick, but Olga was quicker. 'That's it,' she squeaked. 'That's it! That's what we'll do with the pool.'

'What do you mean, "That's what *we'll* do with the pool"?' demanded Noel suspiciously. He didn't like the way Olga was looking at him.

Olga gave a deep sigh. She sometimes wished guinea-pigs weren't quite so intelligent compared to other creatures. There was such a wide gap it did make explaining things a little difficult at times. She would simply have to be patient.

'There's the pool,' she began, as slowly and as distinctly as she could manage. 'Now, you all know that. It's just down the garden by the rockery. It's a big hole in the ground and it's usually full of water, only at the moment it isn't . . .'

'Oh, *do* get on with it,' hissed Noel.

Olga ignored the unseemly interruption. 'If Mr Sawdust had taken Venables and all the fish out of it and pumped the water into the bath it must mean that it's started to leak and that's why all the water is disappearing. It's probably been doing it for a long time, only no one has noticed it before. Some of us, mentioning no names,' she added meaningly, but staring hard at Noel, 'never notice *anything.*'

'Now, if we can fill the hole with something to stop the water running out – like some old pieces of bread – we shall save the world!'

'But I haven't got any bread,' wailed Fangio. 'I don't get it every day. It's a special treat.'

'I *never* get it,' said Graham. 'Not that I mind. I don't like bread.'

'How about bran and oats?' said Noel with a wicked gleam in his eye.

'They would be no good,' said Olga firmly. 'No good at all. If they were you'd be welcome to all I have, but I know they wouldn't be any good. I get the bits in my water bowl sometimes and they just float. No, what we need is something special ... something that goes really hard when it dries, like ...' – she gazed out at the others in search of inspiration and, as her eyes alighted on Noel, it suddenly came to her–' ... like your Pussy's Pleasure.'

'That's a good idea,' said Graham. 'I've heard Mrs Sawdust grumbling sometimes when she's been washing your bowl.'

'Trying to, more like,' agreed Fangio. 'I heard her going on about it the other morning when I went past the kitchen. She said your Pussy's Pleasure had gone as hard as concrete on the sides.'

Graham and Fangio looked up at Olga admiringly. 'I wish I got ideas like that,' said Graham.

'Now, look here ...' began Noel.

'You know you don't like it,' said Fangio. 'It'll be a good chance to get rid of it.'

While the others were talking Olga had a quick nibble from her bowl of bran and oats and then sat back listening. She was tempted to chip in and say that the sooner Noel's Pussy's Pleasure was out of the way the better, but wisely she resisted the temptation. She was content to let Graham and Fangio argue her case for her.

Really, things couldn't have worked out better, and she quite saw what Graham meant when he said he wished he could have ideas like hers. She sometimes wondered where on earth they came from herself.

Noel's Pussy's Pleasure had been a subject for discussion in the Sawdust family's household for several weeks past, ever since it had first been advertised on television as the biggest breakthrough in cat food since frozen fish.

One evening Mr Sawdust had arrived home staggering beneath the weight of a large cardboard box full of tins, having taken advantage of a bargain offer in the local supermarket.

At first Noel, who was very set in his ways

when it came to food and hated any kind of change, had treated the matter with the contempt it deserved. Unlike the cat who appeared in the television commercial, and whose excitement whenever a bowl of Pussy's Pleasure came within sniffing distance was such that it practically had to be put into a strait-jacket, he'd tried to ignore the whole thing. If the Sawdust family wanted to waste their money that was up to them.

But lately, faced with the prospect of either eating it or going without he'd taken to having the occasional snack.

However, the thought of having to get through a whole cardboard box of it filled him with gloom, and even the news that the Sawdust family would be able to send off for a new feeding bowl with his name on the side in return for ten labels from the tins didn't make the taste any better.

'All right,' he said at last. 'You win. At least it'll be better than *eating* the stuff.'

Once he'd made up his mind, Noel lost no time in putting Olga's plan into action and for the next half an hour or so his pussy flap was

put to good use as he hurried back and forth
between the kitchen and the pool.

While Noel was busy doing this, Graham and
Fangio made their way down the garden so that
they could watch the proceedings from the edge
of the pool and give encouragement when
needed.

By squeezing herself against the side of her
dining-room and pressing her nose hard against
the wire netting, Olga was able to get a grand-
stand view of it all and she felt well pleased with
the way things had turned out.

She was just wondering if she might get
another medal to go with the one she'd once
received for saving the Sawdust family's house
from burning down, when she was brought
back to earth by Mr Sawdust's voice. A very

cross Mr Sawdust by the sound of it. He didn't seem at all pleased.

'What on earth's going on?' he cried. 'There's blessed cat food everywhere. Look at it!'

He came outside the kitchen and stared down the garden. 'And what's Noel doing in the pool? Treading all over my wet cement . . . I'll show him . . . I'll teach him to bury his Pussy's Pleasure all over my new fountain. I haven't even tested it yet. It'll be Pussy's Doom by the time I've finished.'

While he was talking Mr Sawdust picked up the end of a length of hosepipe coiled up on the concrete and disappeared into the kitchen again. A moment later there was a hiss from somewhere inside and the hosepipe began jumping about like a thing possessed.

There was a pause as it settled down again and then, before Olga's astonished gaze, there came a spluttering noise and a column of water shot up from the centre of the pool, carrying all before it. A moment later, as the water died down, there was a soft patter patter as Noel's dinner rained back down to earth. But the sound was short lived, for almost immediately

36

it was drowned by a screech from Noel; a screech of mingled surprise and rage as the truth dawned on him, and it was echoed in part by

Graham and Fangio as they tried to scramble clear.

Olga backed away from her front door as

Noel, looking for all the world like a drowned rat, came stalking back up the garden and paused by her hutch. For once she was glad to be safely behind her wire netting.

'How was I to know Mr Sawdust was putting a fountain in the pool?' she squeaked. 'You're the one who always knows what's going on. It *could* have been a leak in the world.'

'That was my dinner,' hissed Noel. 'My dinner. Blown to smithereens.'

'You'll just have to try catching a few mice for a change,' said Olga primly. 'It'll do you good.'

'Mice!' The look Noel gave Olga as he made for his pussy flap had to be seen to be believed.

A moment later he was back outside again.

'Oh, no you don't,' said a voice. 'You're not coming indoors in that state.'

Noel opened his mouth and then gave a start as something landed on the end of his nose. It could have been some more of his dinner, only it wasn't.

'Rain!' he said bitterly. 'That's all I need.'

Olga hurried to her door. 'That's all any of us

need,' she squeaked. 'Now there'll be some nice green grass again. Wheeeeee!

'Perhaps,' she added brightly, 'your dinner going up into the sky like that started it off. I expect it hasn't rained for so long it's forgotten how. When it saw your dinner going everywhere, it remembered. I'll tell you a story if you like . . .'

'Pah!' said Noel, and he stalked off in search of a sheltering bush.

'Wheeeeee!' said Olga sadly, addressing anyone who happened to be listening. 'Wheeeeeeeeee!'

Really, it was very difficult pleasing her friends all the time – or even some of the time. And with certain of them, mentioning no names but it began with 'N', there was no pleasing them at all!

## CHAPTER THREE

## *Olga and the Sponsored Squeak*

Olga was in a jam. In fact, that day she had been in a number of different jams, each worse than the one before, until her mind was in such a whirl she didn't know which way to turn.

*Not*, she would have been at pains to point out, that she *could* have turned even if she'd wanted to, for at that particular moment she was wedged – there was really no other word for it – *wedged* into the cardboard box normally reserved for her visits to the vet, and en route to goodness knew where.

What made matters worse was that it was all happening without so much as a by-your-leave.

The day had begun in its usual leisurely manner, with a breakfast of bran and oats and a handful of grass, all washed down by some fresh, clear water. Then, because it was 'cleaning-out' day, she'd been put in her run on the lawn for an extra feed.

Olga always liked days out on the lawn. There was nothing quite the same as grass you'd chosen yourself, fresh, juicy and just right for nibbling. Not to mention the possibility of stumbling across the odd dandelion leaf or piece of clover, and after the dry spring Mr Sawdust's lawn once again had an ample supply of both. He'd tried to get rid of them by putting down something called 'weedkiller', but there had been so much protesting on her behalf from the rest of the family he'd never tried it again.

And quite right, too. Olga could never understand humans and the way they carried on, often destroying what was best in the world just because they felt it 'didn't look nice'. Olga remembered the incident well because she hadn't been allowed out for several weeks afterwards; not until the dandelions and clover had all died.

Her mind was full of these and other thoughts when she happened to hear her name mentioned. She pricked up her ears at once.

'I bet Olga could do it,' came Karen Sawdust's voice. 'I bet Olga could do it better than anyone else's guinea-pig.'

Olga nodded approvingly. She had no idea what they were talking about but whatever it was she felt sure Karen was right and she could do it better.

'You should hear the way she goes on sometimes when she's hungry,' continued Karen Sawdust. 'You can hear her for miles.'

'Hear me for miles,' Olga repeated to herself. 'What *can* they be on about?'

And then all was revealed. It seemed that Karen and some friends had got together and were organizing a sponsored squeak for all the guinea-pigs in the neighbourhood. It had to do with something called a charity in aid of other animals who weren't quite so lucky, and as far as Olga could make out people were being asked to guess which guinea-pig would have the longest and loudest squeak.

There was no doubt in her mind as to who that would be. In fact, she was so excited by the idea she let out one of her loudest ever squeaks. It was so loud it brought the others dashing to the side of her run.

'Olga!' cried Karen Sawdust. 'Are you all right?'

'*Am* I all right?' Olga gave another squeak. 'Wheeeeeeeeeeeeeeeeee! I was only showing you, that's all.'

And with that she settled down to more eating. If she was going in for something special that evening, like a sponsored squeak, she would need all her strength.

Olga spent the rest of the day 'conserving her strength'. So much so that when the time came for the Sawdust family to set off she was fast asleep, and her squeals were so loud when she was woken up and put into the cardboard box they threatened to wake the entire neighbourhood.

'If she keeps that up,' said Mr Sawdust, 'we'll be home and dry.'

'The people I feel sorry for,' agreed Mrs Sawdust, 'are those who've put their money on the other guinea-pigs. They won't stand a chance.'

As the memory of where she was going slowly came back to her, Olga sat in the bottom of the box preening herself, only giving vent to a very occasional squeak – just to make sure her voice was still working.

Gradually the warmth and motion of the car brought on a feeling of drowsiness again and she was just settling back in her hay so that she could enjoy the ride when it happened: the first of the jams.

One moment they were driving merrily along, enjoying the evening sunshine; the next moment it went very dark and the car came to a halt.

It had to do with something called a 'rush hour' and according to Mr Sawdust it was a 'blessed nuisance', for it meant they were stuck under a railway bridge.

Olga was just thinking it was yet another example of human strangeness – calling something a 'rush hour' when all you did was sit and wait, when there was a roar from somewhere overhead and the whole ground shook. Worse still, it was followed almost immediately by another clattering roar, this time going in the opposite direction.

'Do you think you ought to see if she's all right?' asked Mr Sawdust.

'There, there.' Karen Sawdust reached down and patted Olga as she cowered in her box. 'Don't worry. It's only a train!'

Olga gazed up at Karen Sawdust as if she could hardly believe her ears, which she couldn't. How *could* she say it? How could she say such a thing when only a few weeks before she'd said quite the opposite.

Olga remembered the occasion very clearly because she'd been on her way to the vet to have her toe-nails cut, something she always hated, when – and it may even have been under the very same bridge – they had been caught in a traffic jam, just as they were now, and a train had passed overhead. At the time it had been so loud and so fearsome Olga had let out a squeal of terror.

Afterwards, Karen had given her a long lecture on the subject, telling her that if you happened to be under a bridge when a train went over it was considered *very* unlucky indeed to say anything at all until someone had asked you a question. Karen had clearly felt very strongly about it, so much so that Olga had spent a sleepless night wondering what was going to happen to her. In the event nothing did, but it had been a narrow escape.

Now, here they were, stuck under a bridge and not one but *two* trains had passed over. Her lips were doubly sealed, which meant she would need to be asked two questions before she could open them again. And all this on a night when she needed her lips to open wider than ever before.

But there was worse to come. In the excitement of the moment Mr Sawdust missed his chance in the traffic and got stuck in the wrong lane. During the long wait that followed Olga counted four more trains passing overhead.

Four! That meant she needed to be asked ... Olga wished she was better at sums and in the end had to resort to counting pieces of hay ... it must mean she had to be asked no less than *six* questions. Then, and only then, could she open her mouth to speak.

And the Sawdust family weren't helping at all, for although they kept asking each other questions they weren't talking to *her*.

'She's looking very strange,' said Mrs Sawdust leaning over the back of her seat to take a closer look. 'Very strange.'

'The sooner we get out of here the better,' said Mr Sawdust. 'Blessed traffic.'

Olga couldn't have agreed more.

'Are you all right, Olga?'

'Phew!' Olga just managed to stifle a squeak of delight as Karen Sawdust bent down to speak to her at long last. One down and five to go.

'She doesn't seem to want to answer,' began Karen Sawdust. 'I do hope she hasn't lost her . . .' The rest of the words were lost as there was a loud rumble overhead.

'Sorry,' called Mr Sawdust as they began to move again at long last. 'I couldn't hear for the noise of that train.'

Olga sank back into the hay, her hopes well and truly dashed. Now she was back to six again!

The rest of the journey was like a nightmare. Although the Sawdust family were plainly worried about her condition, try as she might Olga couldn't get them to ask her about it. She tried jumping about in her box, even climbing up the side pretending she was trying to escape, but it was all in vain. Once or twice, when Mr Sawdust went round a corner, she took advantage of the fact and seized the opportunity to roll over on her side, but that only resulted in Mr Sawdust being told off for driving too fast. The last time she tried it on was as they went over a bump going through some gates to where THE EVENT was due to take place, but in her desperation she overdid it and rolled right over on to her back where she lay with her legs sticking up in the air, looking most undignified.

It was all she could do not to cry out. All the same, it did produce three questions – all in a row.

'Olga!' cried Karen Sawdust anxiously. 'What *are* you doing?

'Look at the state of your fur. How could you at a time like this?

'What *is* the matter with you?'

Olga couldn't answer any of the questions, but at least she was halfway to being able to, *and* there would be no more railway bridges to get stuck under.

Because of the delay they were the last to arrive and, as Olga was lifted out of her box, the air was already full of excited squeaks from the other guinea-pigs. But they only served to make her feel even more miserable. Oh, dear, what *was* she to do?

She brightened slightly as Karen Sawdust chose that moment to ask her exactly the same question. 'Oh dear, Olga,' she said. 'What *are* we going to do?'

Normally Olga would have replied with a very loud squeak indeed, but the nearer the time came for the judging the more determined she was that on no account would she go back on her decision to follow Karen Sawdust's instructions about bridges and trains down to the very last letter. She'd managed to get so far and now wild horses wouldn't have made her change her mind. Olga could be very stubborn when she chose.

'Why not try shaking her?' suggested someone, as they came to see what the matter was. 'Perhaps her squeak's stuck.'

Someone else near by gave voice to what struck Olga as a very coarse laugh indeed. 'Try holding her up by her tail. Tee! Hee! Hee!'

'How *can* they make silly jokes at a time like this?' she thought.

And then she felt rather than saw someone else approaching. Someone important, because everyone else stopped talking. Yes, he had a white coat on. It must be the man in charge. And still she had two more questions to go.

The next moment she felt herself being picked up again, gently but firmly.

'Well, now,' said the man, giving her a poke with his finger. 'And who have we here?'

Olga took a deep breath and thought one of her hardest ever thoughts in the hope that something would happen. 'I'm Olga da Polga,' she thought. 'And I could out-squeak anyone here

51

if only I was allowed to, but I've still got another question to go and now I'm never going to be able to because it's going to be too late and . . .'

And then it happened. Karen Sawdust and the judge both spoke at once.

'You're a funny sort of chap,' said the man, as he went to put her down. 'The strong, silent type.'

And, 'Olga,' groaned Karen Sawdust, 'how *can* you be so difficult?'

Olga's indignation knew no bounds. Relieved from her bonds at long last she raised her head, opened her mouth, and gave vent to the loudest, the most piercing squeak she had ever uttered in the whole of her life.

'Wheeeeeeeeeeeeeeeeeeeeeeeeeeeeeeeeeeeeeee- eeeeeeeeeeeeeeeeee!' she went. '*Chap*! *Difficult*! I'm not a *chap*, wheeeeeeeeeeeeeeeeee! And as for being *difficult* . . .' she took an even deeper breath and gave another squeak, and then another and another.

'Well,' said the man, when he'd recovered himself. 'We don't have to look any further, do we?'

But this time Olga didn't answer. 'I may,' she
decided, 'keep some questions in reserve.' She
had a lot to tell the others when she got home.
'And who knows?' she thought. 'I might get
stuck under one of those blessed railway bridges
again on the way back. Then what would happen?'

## CHAPTER FOUR

# Olga's Dream House

One evening Olga came to her front door and let out two loud squeaks. The first one was short and sharp. Then she took a deep breath and gave another, much longer one.

To an ordinary passer-by there was nothing remarkable in this. Olga often squeaked. Usually it meant she was hungry.

But another guinea-pig, or any of the other animal inhabitants who happened to be within earshot, would have known at once that something was wrong.

To start with, Olga wasn't making sense,

which was most unusual, for she never wasted her squeaks on trifles. The first one sounded like 'FANGEY' and the second, much longer one, sounded for all the world like 'O'SHIDE-AWAY', and it was said in tones of total and utter disgust.

All was not well with Olga.

The troubles had started several days before and had to do with dogs, or rather with one dog in particular – a fearsome hound called Dagwood.

Dagwood was staying as a 'house guest' with the family next door. At least, that's what the Sawdust family's neighbours called him. Mr Sawdust called him something else. What it meant Olga wasn't sure, but whatever it was she heartily agreed with the tone in which it was said, for Dagwood was a pest. Neither she nor any of her friends had been given a moment's peace ever since he'd arrived on the scene. As far as she was concerned, '*garden* guest' would have been a much better description – or even 'garden *pest*'. Dagwood's heavy breathing and his snorts of frustration as he dashed hither and thither on the other side of the fence trying to find a way through had to be heard to be believed.

Matters had come to a head that afternoon when, unable to contain himself a moment longer, he'd dug a tunnel underneath some boards and into the Sawdust family's garden.

As ill luck would have it Fangio had been passing at the time and he'd received the brunt of the attack, plus a very severe shock into the bargain.

Unlike most hedgehogs, Fangio often came

out for a stroll during the day. He liked a chat, particularly before he began his night's work, but on this occasion he got far more than he'd bargained for.

Fortunately, before Dagwood actually sank his teeth into him, Fangio managed to roll himself up into a ball, but it had been a very nasty moment indeed.

After chasing Noel up a tree, Dagwood turned his attention to Graham. But Graham was more than ready for him. He simply withdrew his head into his shell and pretended he was a passing stone.

More frustrated than ever, Dagwood had then set upon Olga and, as she'd been at pains to tell the others at every opportunity since, it had been a terrifying experience. One moment she'd been enjoying a quiet nibble on the lawn, the next moment there had been a roar and a deafening crash as Dagwood landed on top of her run, barking fit to wake the dead. She could still feel his hot breath on her face as he scrabbled at the grass, trying to force a way under, and she shuddered to think what might have happened had he succeeded.

Fortunately by then the noise had brought the Sawdust family running and before he had a chance to do anything of the sort they'd come to the rescue and he'd been driven off.

The chase had taken him through the middle of Mr Sawdust's vegetable garden, over the rockery, through several flower beds, over the strawberry patch, and finally into the pond. The crowning insult came as he scrambled out again and then shook himself dry over everybody. The trail of damage he left behind had taken Mr Sawdust several days' hard work to put right.

All the animals agreed that *something* would have to be done, but none of them knew quite what.

All eyes turned towards Noel. Cats being the traditional enemy of dogs, they felt sure he would have some ideas on the matter. But Noel would have none of it. Although he left the others in no doubt as to what would happen next time he and Dagwood came face to face, he obviously had no intention of seeking out an early meeting.

'I've got much more important things to do,' he announced in superior tones, punctuating his remark with a bang from his pussy flap as he disappeared indoors rather faster than usual.

There the affair was left, and as it happened it was just as well, for the very next day Mr Sawdust himself decided to take over.

Olga had barely finished breakfast when Karen and her father arrived outside the house laden with all sorts of bits and pieces.

They came and went several times, first to the

garden shed, then to somewhere called a 'Do-it-Yourself Shop', and after that to the garage. Each time they arrived back they were carrying something new.

Finally, Mr Sawdust went indoors and came out again carrying his toolbox and a large book.

'Right,' he said. 'We'll just check we've got everything, then we can start work.'

Olga sat listening as Mr Sawdust's voice droned on. 'Thirty feet of four by three-quarters – prepared. Fifteen feet of two by one. Polythene sheet. Wire netting. One inch pipe. Elbow. Backnuts. Nails ...'

Each time Mr Sawdust called out an item from his list, Karen Sawdust gave an answering 'yes'.

'Bacon rind ...'

'Mummy said she'd let us have some later,' replied Karen.

'Good. We mustn't forget it.'

'Bacon rind!' Olga, who'd nearly nodded off to sleep gave a squeak of surprise. What *was* going on? What could they be making?

The thought was hardly out of her mind when the answer came.

'It's going to be a lovely house,' said Karen Sawdust. 'And safe as anything.'

'And air-conditioned,' said Mr Sawdust proudly, as he picked up some of the wood. 'Don't forget that.'

As Mr Sawdust and Karen disappeared round the side of the house in order to do some sawing, Olga sank back into her hay with a look of rapture on her face.

She had no idea what 'air-conditioned' meant, but it sounded very special indeed. Perhaps it had something to do with her fur. Perhaps they'd meant 'fur-conditioned'; not that her fur needed anything doing to it. But that was only a minor detail. The important thing was she was going to have a new house. Trust the Sawdust family to make sure she was kept safe and sound and free from attack. There was no doubt about it, ever since she'd been with them she'd been properly looked after. Food, water, hay for her bedroom; she'd never once been left to want.

On the other hand, she *had* been with them for quite a long time. Olga wasn't sure how long. There had certainly been several summers, and winters, too; not to mention the bits in between, and her hutch, nice though it was, hadn't altered in all that time.

She wondered what her new house would look like. Perhaps it would be very grand and have a moat and a drawbridge like the one she had once stayed in with Boris.

Boris . . . a dreamy look came over her face as she thought of Boris, and of her family – long since departed.

On the other hand, it would need a very big moat indeed to keep out a dog the size of Dagwood. As it was he'd practically filled the pond. She wasn't too sure about a moat if it was going to be that big, for it would mean she would be a long way away from all that was going on. Far better to have some special wire with spikes in. Olga liked to see what was going on, and as if to prove her point she peered out of her front door in order to see how her new house was progressing.

The hammering and sawing had been growing louder all the time and the comings and goings more frequent.

Mr Sawdust was busying himself with a paint brush. 'It's some special stuff that preserves the wood but doesn't smell,' he explained to Karen Sawdust. 'They hate the smell of creosote.'

Olga nodded her agreement. She knew all about creosote from when Mr Sawdust had painted the fence near her hutch one day. The smell had been so strong it had put her off her food for several days.

Having finished off the painting, Mr Sawdust picked up what was obviously one of the most important parts of the operation – the fitting of what he called the entrance tunnel.

'There,' he said, as he hammered a long, square-looking wooden object into place, 'that should keep any intruders out!'

'Do you think we ought to have taken some

measurements first?' asked Karen Sawdust. 'It wouldn't do for "a certain person" to get stuck.'

'Get stuck! Wheeeeee!' Olga gave an indignant squeak as the words sank in. Fancy suggesting she might get stuck! She was so upset she missed Mr Sawdust's reply, and it was with a mixture of surprise and disappointment that she watched them pick up the new house between them and carry it off down the garden.

It was a very strange looking affair. As far as she could make out there weren't any windows in it at all. It was simply a large square box with the entrance tunnel sticking out at one end like a long neck, and with what looked like a tail made of piping at the other.

She hoped they weren't going to put it too far down the garden. Being kept safe was one thing; being too far away to call for help was quite another matter. Besides, she liked being near the house – it was where everything happened and it was nice to be able to keep a watchful eye on the comings and goings.

All the same, she felt very excited at the trouble that was being taken on her behalf and she couldn't wait to tell the others all about it.

But the others, for reasons best known to themselves, were nowhere to be seen.

Karen Sawdust came back up the garden several times, first for a spade and a wheelbarrow, then for the sheet of black polythene and finally for the mysterious pieces of bacon rind.

'What they can possibly want *that* for, goodness only knows,' thought Olga. Her diet was a strictly vegetarian one and the very thought of eating any form of meat made her feel positively sick.

But when she came out of her bedroom again, having got over the thought, everything had gone quiet. Mr Sawdust and Karen had gone back indoors and even Dagwood was silent for a change.

It was all most disappointing after the earlier excitement. Perhaps they were waiting for the paint to dry properly before letting her see her new house ... perhaps the bacon rind was meant to keep Dagwood away ... perhaps ... Olga closed her eyes and began dreaming about the grand new life she was about to lead. The others would be able to come and visit her from time to time and she would be able to tell them all about it. Perhaps she ought to be thinking up some stories she could tell them to be going on with ...

It was late that same evening when a bang from Noel's pussy flap brought her awake with a start.

'Wheeee!' she squeaked. 'Wheeeeeeeeee! Have you heard? Mr Sawdust and Karen have been building a special house. It's like a castle. It's got a special tunnel and air-conditioning and ...'

Noel gave a yawn and stretched himself. 'I know. I've heard nothing else all the evening. Plans everywhere. Nowhere to lie down. I've never heard so much fuss. If you ask me there are *some* who are very lucky. The rest of us have got to take pot luck ...'

'I'll let you come in,' said Olga, knowing full well she would do no such thing when it came down to it. It wasn't that she didn't trust Noel, it was just that ... well, she didn't *altogether* trust him.

Noel gave her a funny look. '*You'll* let me come and see it?' he repeated. 'Do you know what they're calling it?'

'No, I don't,' said Olga. She was getting rather fed up with the way Noel seemed to know so much more about it all than she did.

'They bought a lot of special letters,' said Noel, 'and they're sorting them out now. Mr Sawdust is going to screw them on to the entrance in the morning. They're calling it FANGEY O'SHIDEAWAY.'

'Fangey O'Shideaway?' repeated Olga. 'I don't think much of that as a name for a house.'

But Noel had gone on his way, anxious to take advantage of the fact that by now Dagwood would be safely locked in for the night.

Olga tried running the words round her tongue again.

'Fan ... geoshide ... away. Fangeyoshide ... away ...' And then it came to her, and as the realization gradually sank in her squeak of indignation knew no bounds. 'Wheeeeeeeeee! How could they? How dare they? Wheeeeeeeeee!' She was so upset she could hardly get the words out of her mouth. 'FAN-GIO'S HIDEAWAY!'

Fancy building a house for a hedgehog. The very idea!

And to show just how cross she was, she went straight to bed and didn't speak to anyone again until the morning. By which time, being a guinea-pig, she'd practically forgotten all about the matter.

CHAPTER FIVE

# *The Battle of Mulberry Hill*

Olga often felt that one of the best things about
living with the Sawdust family was that they
had a particularly nice garden. She'd seen some
of the others in the neighbourhood and as far as
she was concerned they were nowhere near as

good. Mr Sawdust was a keen gardener and apart from the lawn there was a sizeable shrubbery – which Graham and Fangio made much use of (although this was something of a mixed blessing when they were needed in a hurry and couldn't be found). Then there was the pond with its fountain and its waterfalls, and several flower beds, not to mention a vegetable patch which was good for lettuce leaves – especially on days when it was too wet for the Sawdust family to go out in search of grass for her.

But undoubtedly the pride and joy of Mr Sawdust's life was a large mulberry tree which stood on a slight hillock in the middle of the lawn. Olga could never quite see why everyone went on about it so, but go on about it they did. Whenever anyone new came to the house they were always taken out into the garden in order to see it, and if the 'ooh's' and 'aah's' were anything to go by, most of them shared Mr Sawdust's delight.

As far as Olga could make out, it was much more trouble than it was worth. It was large and very old – so much so that some of the heavier branches had to be propped up in case they snapped, and the fruit was so high it could only be picked with the aid of a ladder. Usually, by the time the family got around to doing it most had been 'got at' by the birds. Apart from that, by then the fruit was so heavy – not unlike giant raspberries – that any movement from the ladder made it fall off and burst on hitting the ground, where it left a nasty stain which lasted for days and days.

Olga wouldn't have minded quite so much if it had been nice to eat, but the one time she tried nibbling a mulberry she'd found it so sour it had made her squeak with surprise, and she'd had a nasty pain in her inside for several days afterwards.

However, all this was a seasonal thing which happened once a year in the late summer. For most of the time the mulberry tree just stood there, shedding its leaves or growing new ones, and if Olga thought about it at all it was really only to feel grateful for its shade when she was out on the lawn and the sun was high in the sky, as it was at the moment, or for its shelter when she got caught in a sudden shower of rain.

Little did she dream that one day that very

same tree would turn her into a heroine for a brief period of time, and cause even Noel to look at her with new respect.

Like many of her adventures it came about in a rather strange and unexpected way.

One morning she was outside in her run on the lawn, trying to decide between nibbles of grass whether to carry on for a while or take shelter in the built-in part at the end until someone came out to move her to a fresh patch (there was quite a breeze blowing and it was ruffling her whiskers more than somewhat), when she felt rather than saw something moving close by.

Instinctively she stopped nibbling and sat very still, hardly daring to breathe. Although she knew from past experience that she was reasonably safe in her run, you never knew.

On the far side of the lawn Noel lay stretching out his paws in a luxurious manner as he drank in the warmth of the sun through half closed eyes. Nearer at hand Olga could see the familiar, but equally dormant rounded hump of Graham. She gave a sniff. Fat lot of good either of them would be in time of trouble.

Then, just as she was about to relax it

happened again – only this time it felt even closer.

Suddenly she saw it – a wiggly object, almost as fat as it was long, coming over the brow of the hill at the foot of the mulberry tree. It was so fat it was impossible to see its eyes, or its legs for that matter. But what really made Olga catch her breath was its colour, or rather its lack of colour, for it was a ghastly white from the top of its head to the very uttermost tip of its tail. Even as she watched, the creature was joined by a second one, and together they came down the slope towards her in a series of short hops, looking for all the world like some primeval slugs which had crawled out of the woodwork after

being hidden from the light of day since the world began.

Not that Olga had time to consider the matter. One glance was enough to send her scurrying for the comparative safety of the shelter at the end of her run, letting out squeaks of terror as she went. Once there, she buried her nose in the furthermost corner and lay quaking and shivering as she waited for the worst to happen.

'Wheeeeee! Wheeeeeeeeee!' Her squeaks grew louder still as a shadow darkened the floor of her shelter. Perhaps the creatures expanded when they saw the sun for the first time. 'Wheeeeeeeeee! Perhaps ...'

'What *is* going on? What's the matter now?' A plaintive meeow from Noel brought Olga back to earth.

'What's the matter?' repeated Olga. '*What's the matter*? Can't you see?'

Taking advantage of Noel's presence she ventured out of her corner and gazed through the wire netting at the lawn beyond, her nose twitching as she tried to catch the scent of the invaders from outer space. For now that her vivid imagination had seized on the problem, that was what she had convinced herself they must be. Invaders from outer space. It was the *only* explanation, for she had never, ever seen anything like them on earth before. She'd sometimes heard Karen Sawdust talking about things from outer space with her friends when she was being cleaned out – usually after they'd been to something called a cinema, but never in her wildest dreams had she expected to come face to face with such beings.

'Wheeeee! Look behind you,' she squeaked, as some more white objects appeared on the brow of the hill.

Noel half turned and then paused, arching his back and stretching out his claws in one continuous movement. For a second or two he remained perfectly motionless; but for a sudden scurry of wind ruffling his fur, he could have been made of stone. Then he pounced on the nearest object. But quick though he was, he wasn't quick enough. Almost before his feet had left the ground his quarry gave a sideways hop and he missed it by a yard.

Olga gave a squeak of fear. Her worst suspicions were confirmed. Anything that could beat Noel to the pounce must be special indeed. As he looked at her sheepishly over his shoulder, pretending he'd only intended to have a wash anyway, she put on one of her 'I told you so' looks. But it was an 'I told you so' look which also said 'I wish I *didn't* have to tell you, and watch out! There's another one right behind you'.

Noel stopped licking himself and took another quick look. Normally the sight of all the white objects jumping hither and thither would have been irresistible. Like most cats, he enjoyed nothing better than a good chase, and the longer it went on and the more difficult it was the better he liked it; but something in the urgent tone of Olga's voice communicated itself to him.

'Don't worry,' he said, as he stood up to go, 'you'll be all right in your run.'

'All right in my run!' Olga's squeak grew higher still as Noel's words sank in. She could hardly believe her ears. He was leaving her to her fate. 'Wheeeee! Wheeeeeeeeeeeeeeeeeeeeeee!'

But her cries had quite the wrong effect on Noel. Any hopes she may have had that they would make him change his mind were dashed as he disappeared in the direction of the house. In fact, if anything, they made him quicken his pace and, in his haste, he almost trod on Graham, who was heading in the direction of

Olga's run in order to see what all the fuss was about.

'You could try using Graham as a barricade,' he called, before he finally disappeared. 'They'll never get past *him*.' Noel knew all about these things through watching television in the evenings.

'What's going on?' Graham stopped in his tracks, sticking his head out and craning his neck to and fro as he surveyed the scene.

'Oh, don't just *stand* there,' moaned Olga. 'You heard . . . be a barricade.'

'What's a barricade?' asked Graham.

'Oh, wheeee!' squeaked Olga in desperation. 'Of all the times to ask silly questions. For goodness sake! All you have to do is stand there.'

Graham looked even more confused. 'I do wish you'd make up your mind,' he said plaintively. 'First you say *don't* stand here . . . then you say *do*.' And he put his head back inside his shell while he thought the problem over.

'I'm coming! I'm coming!' Fangio, his prickles sticking out like a porcupine's, came hurrying across the lawn. Looking neither to the right nor to the left, he went straight past the bottom of Olga's run and disappeared into a flower bed on the other side of the garden.

Olga's moans and groans as she rushed up and down reached fever pitch. By now the lawn was covered in white objects as a never-ending stream fanned out across the top of the hillock. They were everywhere. How *could* the others behave in such a way? Deserting her in her hour of need. It was unbelievable. Wheeeeeeee! It . . .

Olga suddenly stopped dead in her tracks as something landed on her head. Her mouth open wide, a squeak which she'd been about to utter cut off before it had even begun, she felt rather than saw a warm trickle of something sticky run down between her eyes and on to her nose.

But before she had a chance to recover, let alone see what was the cause, there came a patter of running feet and Karen Sawdust burst on the scene.

'Olga! Olga!' she cried. 'What *is* going on? What *have* you done to yourself? You're covered in blood. It's all over your face . . .'

'Blood!' What was left in Olga's veins suddenly went cold. 'Blood? All over my face? Wheeeeugh!' The cry of anguish changed into a gurgle as she felt her run being tipped up and a warm pair of hands took hold of her.

Usually when she was taken out of her run she put up a bit of a struggle. More of a token to show what was what. But for once she was happy to lay back and let things take their course.

She was dimly aware of the jogging motion as Karen Sawdust carried her gently towards the house, past the wide-open eyes of Noel, Fangio and Graham – all of whom had come back to witness the goings on, when she felt all dizzy and everything seemed to go black.

Olga never knew how long it lasted, but when she came round again she found she was back in her own house, all clean and tidy and lying in a rucked up pile of soft hay. The sticky feeling on her nose had gone and although it still felt wet, the strange smell that had accompanied it had gone too.

She looked around to make sure everything was in its proper place – her bowl of water and her bowl of oats, and then she peered out through the front door.

To her surprise she was greeted by a chorus of meeows and squeaks and grunts.

'Are you all right?' For once Noel sounded genuinely worried.

'Wheeeeee!' Olga gave a loud squeak of reassurance. Then, because she liked an audience and had a sense of occasion, she added a sort of groan for good measure. She was really quite pleased with the result.

'It was very brave of you,' said Graham.

'Oh, it was nothing . . .' Olga tried hard to remember what had happened and what it was she was supposed to have done.

'All those THINGS,' persisted Graham. 'They were really after you.'

'I've never seen so much blood,' agreed

Fangio. 'Not since Mr Sawdust hit himself with the hammer.'

'*And* he made a lot more fuss,' broke in Graham, anxious not to be outdone. 'He jumped up and down so he nearly trod on me.'

'Oh, it was nothing.' A faraway look came into Olga's eyes as the morning's events gradually came back to her and she felt the beginnings of a story enter her mind. 'I'll tell you all about it if you like.'

She took a deep breath. 'I shall call it the Battle of Mulberry Hill, because it all took place under the mulberry tree. Some of you may want to sit down while you listen,' she added, casting a meaning glance in Noel's direction.

'There's rather a lot of blood in it and you may find it upsetting particularly if you don't happen to be very brave yourself.'

Noel opened his mouth as if he was about to say something, but before he had a chance to the kitchen door opened.

'Good gracious!' Mrs Sawdust took in the scene. 'What *is* going on?'

'It's one of those days,' said Karen Sawdust. 'What with all that plastic packing Daddy's new Hi-Fi came in blowing away . . .' She bent down and picked something up off the ground. 'I wonder if that's what frightened Olga? It's funny stuff. Just like a lot of white worms.'

'It's very light,' agreed Mrs Sawdust. 'No wonder it went everywhere. We'd better pick it up before it gets any worse . . .'

'Poor Olga.' Karen Sawdust poked a finger through Olga's front door. 'Fancy having a mulberry fall on to your head into the bargain. No wonder you were upset. We were too. The way it burst made it look as if you were covered in blood.'

'As I was saying,' continued Olga hastily as Karen Sawdust followed her mother down the

garden, 'I've called this story the Battle of Mulberry Hill . . .'

But it was too late, her audience was already
melting away.

'A *mulberry*!' Noel nearly spat the word out
as he leapt up onto a near-by fence and arched
his back in disgust.

Olga turned to the others. 'As I was saying,'
she repeated.

But Graham, showing a surprising turn of
speed, was already on his way, and Fangio was
busying himself with the remains of some bread
and milk he'd found.

Olga gave a sigh and turned her attention to

her bowl of oats. It had promised to be a good story and really, now she came to think of it, one which would probably have been wasted on the others.

Perhaps she would save it to tell to herself some time, but later, after she'd had a good sleep.

'After all,' thought Olga to herself, 'it's so exciting that if I told it to myself now I might *never* get to sleep.' And with that she disappeared into her bedroom and wasn't seen for the rest of the day.

## CHAPTER SIX

# *Who's a Pretty Girl, then?*

'Who's a pretty girl, then? Who's a pretty girl?'

Olga, who as it happened was busy gazing at her own reflection in the water bowl, preened herself as Mrs Sawdust's voice floated out through her kitchen door.

It was a silly question, of course, since the answer was so obvious it was hardly worth asking in the first place. All the same, it gave her a nice warm glow to feel that others were thinking of her.

Clearly, Mrs Sawdust had a friend in for what

was known as 'morning coffee', for almost immediately another, gruffer voice which she didn't recognize, said exactly the same thing.

'Who's a pretty girl, then? Who's a pretty girl?'

'Wheeeeeeee!' said Olga. 'Wheeeeeeeeee! Wheeeeeeeeeeee!' There was no harm in letting the others know she was up and about and agreed with everything they were saying.

'Who's a *clever* girl, then? Who's a *clever* girl?'

'Wheeeeeeee!' squeaked Olga. 'Yes, that's true, too.'

'Who's a *clever* girl, then?' Again the same gruff voice repeated what Mrs Sawdust had said.

'How about coming out for a little while?' asked Mrs Sawdust.

'Wheeeeee!' said Olga. 'Thank you very much.'

She took one final glance at her reflection and then stretched herself in readiness. She hadn't expected to go out on the lawn quite so early in the morning, on the other hand it was a nice day and there was really no reason not to.

Mrs Sawdust said something else, but she

couldn't tell what it was for the shrill sound of some dreadful bird screeching, so she contented herself with waiting patiently for someone to come and put her in her run.

There was a bang as Mrs Sawdust closed her kitchen window, and then silence.

After she'd waited for several minutes and still nothing had happened, Olga began to get restive. 'Really,' she thought, 'either people want me to go out on the grass or they don't!' And she was about to let the others know her feelings on the matter when suddenly there was a dreadful commotion inside the kitchen.

There was a series of shrieks and cries and screeches and then Noel's pussy flap popped open and Noel himself shot out as if his very life depended on it; and by the sound of Mrs Sawdust's voice it did just that.

'Wretched cat!' she cried. 'Don't you ever do that again. Poor Josephine!'

Noel landed just a few feet away from Olga's hutch. He sat there for a moment or two and then, sensing that Olga had her beady eyes fixed on him, he had a quick wash as if to pretend that nothing had happened. As he did so a small, blue feather detached itself from his whiskers and floated gently to the ground.

'Just let her wait,' Noel said at last. He paused in his washing and stared at the kitchen door. 'Just let her wait!'

Olga looked most surprised. Although Noel was very independent – or *pretended* he was – Olga sometimes suspected he wasn't quite as independent as he made himself out to be, and it was very unusual for him to have a cross word to say about any of the Sawdust family. Especially Mrs Sawdust, who never let him down when it came to feeding time, or if he was in any kind of trouble.

'Not Mrs Sawdust,' said Noel impatiently, when Olga started questioning him. 'That ... that ... *bird*.' He seemed to have difficulty in getting the word out. 'Fancy having a *bird* in the house. And letting it fly around like that. How was I to know? I thought I was doing them a good turn.'

Noel licked his lips at the memory of it all. 'If it had been any other sort of bird they'd have been pleased if I'd caught it for them. If it had come from outside they would have *asked* me to. Just because it's a budgerigar and it *talks* ...'

'Talks?' Everything began to fall into place. The strange voice in the kitchen. The screeching ... Olga suddenly felt very put out at the thought of there being an addition to the household. A stranger in their midst, without so much as a by-your-leave. One, moreover, that talked ... just like humans.

'What does it say?' she asked, unable to bring

herself to say the word 'she'; half of her was dying to know the answer while the other half felt it would rather not.

'Oh, this and that.' Noel was rapidly losing interest in the subject. He was content to bide his time until the right moment arrived to get his revenge.

Left to her own devices, Olga began to brood on the matter. She viewed the whole affair with very mixed feelings indeed, and when, later that morning, Karen Sawdust came out to 'see to her', she went into her bedroom and didn't utter a word, just to show her displeasure.

When Karen Sawdust went back indoors she heard her telling Mrs Sawdust all about it.

'Olga's in a bad mood this morning,' she said. 'I can't think what's the matter with her. I hope she's not sickening for anything.'

'Perhaps we ought to take her to the vet,' replied Mrs Sawdust. 'Unless, of course, it's jealousy. You never know. Animals are sometimes funny that way.'

'Jealous?' thought Olga. 'Me? *Jealous*? Of a *budgerigar*? How could they?'

As the kitchen door closed she looked around for other ears to unburden herself on.

But if Noel was of little help, the others were even worse.

Talking to Graham was sometimes like talking to a brick wall, particularly if he wasn't interested. At least a brick wall stood still. With Graham, things just bounced off his shell and he went on his way as if nothing had happened.

And just so long as he got his bread and milk occasionally, Fangio couldn't have cared two hoots what went on in the Sawdust family's house. Since he'd got his new house it had taken most of his attention.

'They're still feeding you, aren't they?' he asked.

Olga had to admit they were.

'And cleaning you out?'

Olga nodded.

'Well, then?'

'Well, then,' thought Olga crossly, as Fangio went on his way, 'is all very well, then.'

In the end she had to make do with scraps of information Noel let fall from time to time. That, and an occasional glimpse of Josephine's cage when Mrs Sawdust opened the kitchen window. And as the kitchen window, since Josephine's arrival, was almost always kept tightly shut, and Noel was still biding his time and pretending he had no interest in the matter, it was all very difficult.

Gradually, however, she began to build up a picture of the scene as the pieces of information fell into place like those of a giant jigsaw puzzle.

It seemed that Josephine lived in a cage which hung by a spring from a large stand.

The inside of the cage contained several perches, a ladder, a swing, a mirror, two bells –

which Olga could often hear ringing, and a table-tennis ball.

There was a water bowl for when she was thirsty, and a seed bowl for her food, and when she was tired of that she had a choice of cuttle fish to keep her beak in good condition, things called iodised nibbles to keep her in good health, special grit for the floor of the cage, and millet sprays on Sundays for a special treat.

It made her own list of belongings look very small indeed: two feeding bowls and a twig for her teeth. There was certainly no mirror. She had to make do with her water bowl when she wanted to see her reflection.

Really, it seemed the smaller you were the more you had. Olga remembered Fircone and Raisin, the hamsters; it had been exactly the same with them. Their cage had been full of things.

She felt very disgruntled. 'Really,' she thought, 'it's a wonder she can get inside her cage with all those things.'

And then one morning the inevitable happened. It was almost a repeat of the previous excitement, except that this time the screams

and the shrieks and the screeches were, if any-thing, even louder.

And when Noel came through his pussy flap he was accompanied by a small, blue object which was making most of the noise.

Once outside, the blue object went one way and Noel went the other, and by the time Mrs Sawdust got the door open both had disap-peared.

The Sawdust family rushed down the garden calling Josephine's name, but to no avail.

'That's torn it,' said Karen Sawdust, as they gathered outside the kitchen. 'What are we going to tell Mrs Holmes?'

'She's due back this afternoon,' said Mrs Sawdust.

'Perhaps we could buy her another one,' said Mr Sawdust hopefully.

'It wouldn't be the same,' said Karen Sawdust. 'Besides, she'd have to teach it to talk all over again.'

'That's the trouble with minding other people's pets,' said Mrs Sawdust, as they went indoors. 'It's such a responsibility.'

Olga suddenly felt quite differently about the matter. If only the Sawdust family had *said* they were only looking after Josephine for a neighbour. She wouldn't have minded a bit.

And another thing: if they had only asked her where Josephine was at that moment she could have told them. Instead of which they had all gone rushing off down the garden like wild things. They'd made so much noise it was a wonder they hadn't driven her away out of sheer fright.

As it was she was still perched on the sill outside Olga's bedroom window, looking rather ruffled, but obviously none the worse for her adventure.

Olga came to a decision. She moved back inside her hutch and then very, very gently, began nuzzling her feeding bowl towards her front door. Bran and oats weren't exactly like bird seed. On the other hand, in her present state Josephine might be glad of anything. From past experience Olga knew there was nothing like the sight of food to set your mind at rest.

Having got her bowl as close to the wire netting as possible she sat very still and waited. Sure enough, after a moment or two, Josephine hopped towards her, easing her way along the ledge until she was able to cling to the edge of Olga's front door.

For a while they both stayed absolutely still,

Olga hardly daring to breathe. Then the ringlet of hearts around Josephine's neck stirred as she opened her beak.

'Who's a pretty girl, then?' she said, staring straight at Olga.

Olga preened herself. 'Well,' she thought. 'Since you ask.'

'Who's a *clever* girl, then?' said Josephine, in a voice as clear as a bell. There was no mistaking the words, or who they were meant for.

Olga was just about to tell her when she stiffened as she saw a familiar black shape appear round the side of the shed.

Her mind raced in all directions. She would have to do something. She recognized from the way Noel had frozen into position that he was almost ready to pounce. And she knew from old that when he did there was no one faster.

She took a deep breath. It was now or never.

Her squeak when it came was exactly right. Even if she'd rehearsed it for days and days she couldn't have done it any better. It was loud enough to reach the Sawdust family's kitchen, yet not so loud that it frightened Josephine, for it started quietly and built up towards the end.

It also had just the right amount of urgency. It said all that needed to be said.

'WheeeeeeeEEEEEEEEEEEEEEEE!'

'WheeeeeeeEEEEEEEEEEEEEEEE!' echoed Josephine, intrigued by this new sound.

And 'Thank goodness for that,' said Mrs Sawdust, as she took hold of Josephine and put her back inside her cage.

'Olga,' said Karen Sawdust, 'you're a heroine. You shall have some special groundsel as a treat. I'll go and get some right now.'

'Who'd have believed it?' said Mr Sawdust.

'I wouldn't have for a start,' said Noel, as the Sawdust family went their separate ways

leaving him alone with Olga. 'Fancy doing a thing like that. A *bird*! That could have been my supper.'

'*I* thought she was very nice,' said Olga. 'And *very* intelligent. I could have listened to her all day.

'Which is more,' she added pointedly, staring straight at Noel, 'than I can say for some.'

And with that she pushed her bowl of bran and oats away from the front door and turned her back on the world. Cats were all very well in their way, but they did tend to go on about the same old things all the time. They sometimes couldn't see beyond the next mouse.

Whereas birds – Olga had a whole new outlook on birds. She gazed at her reflection in the water bowl and gave a squeak of approval.

'Wheeeeeeee!' she went. 'Who's a pretty girl, then? Who's a heroine?'

CHAPTER SEVEN

# Olga Goes Jogging

One day Olga was slowly coming awake, peering through her bedroom window at the outside world and wondering whether or not it was worth going out into her dining-room before the early morning dew had disappeared, when she had a great shock.

The door leading to the Sawdust family's kitchen suddenly burst open and Mr Sawdust came out, looked about him rather furtively for a moment or two, and then disappeared round the corner of the house in the direction of the road.

In itself, there was nothing unusual about this. Mr Sawdust came out of the very same door practically every day of the year. On weekdays he was usually dressed in a dark suit and carried a small case under his arm. At weekends and during the holidays it was often much later in the morning and he usually wore older clothes, perhaps a sweater or an open-necked shirt.

But Olga couldn't remember ever having seen him coming out so early, and *never* had she seen him dressed in quite such an odd manner. If *dressed* was the right word. *Un*dressed would be more like it, for he was wearing just a thin white singlet and a pair of very short trousers which showed his knees. Olga had never seen Mr Sawdust's knees before and she tried to get a closer look, but instead of moving in his usual dignified manner he kept jumping up and down, and when he disappeared round the corner of the house it was rather as if he was being pursued by some enormous beast of prey.

Olga was so taken aback she sat with her jaw open for quite some time, her eyes large, round and full of wonder.

She couldn't wait to tell the others, especially

Noel, who, because of his privileged position of being able to come and go through his pussy flap, knew everything that was going on in the Sawdust family's house. Or even if he didn't, he pretended to.

Olga felt sure that this time she would have one up on him, for more often than not Noel slept on in the morning on account of having been up late the night before – a rather sore point because Olga's sleep was sometimes disturbed in the early hours by his comings and goings. If Noel was having a 'field night' with mice, the bangs from his pussy flap sounded like machine-gun fire.

This particular morning was no exception, and the sun was high in the sky by the time he made his first appearance of the day. Mr Sawdust had long since returned from whatever it was he'd been doing, changed into his normal clothes, and left for the office.

But at long last the awaited bang from the pussy flap brought Olga running out into her dining-room. She pressed her nose against the wire netting of her front door and gave a squeak as Noel sauntered past looking for a convenient patch of sunshine where he could enjoy his morning wash before going back to sleep again.

He listened to her excited squeaks for a while and then gave a yawn.

'Is *that* all,' he said. 'That's only jogging. I heard them all talking about it last night before I went out. He'll be doing it every morning from now on.'

Stifling her disappointment, Olga considered the matter for a moment or two. 'I don't see much fun in jigging,' she said at last. 'It sounds like a lot of fuss over nothing.'

'It's *jogging*,' said Noel, 'and it isn't meant to be fun. People do it to keep fit and lose weight. They don't keep themselves in good condition like cats because they don't get enough exercise.'

Noel, thoroughly awake now, went into great detail about all he'd heard the night before.

It was Olga's turn to yawn. 'Well, jigging or jogging,' she said, '*I* don't think much of it.' And she buried her head in her bowl of oats to show that as far as she was concerned the discussion was at an end.

Noel looked rather miffed. 'If anyone needs a good jog you do,' he said, 'stuck in that hutch all day. About the only exercise you get is when you eat. It's a wonder you don't seize up. Not,' he added as a parting shot, 'that you'd be able to jog if you tried. You're so fat, if you jumped up in the air you'd go straight through the floor.'

And with that he arched his back, stretched, and before Olga had time to say any more, moved slowly on his way to follow the sunshine.

'Wheeee!' squeaked Olga, when she'd recovered herself. 'Wheelll, really! Cats!'

And she went back into her bedroom in order

to sleep off the nasty taste the whole affair had left her with.

But as she settled down in her hay she happened to catch sight of her reflection in the window. She gazed at it for a while. The fact of the matter was she hadn't taken a good long look at herself for some while. Looking at her reflection in her water bowl was one thing. That was close to. Seen from a distance she had to admit that there could have been a grain of truth in Noel's remarks. Only the tiniest grain, of course, but she had perhaps put on a little weight here and there. During the summer months she was often put out in her run on the lawn and it could be that she'd been eating a little more grass than usual. It was only natural, for that was the whole idea – it saved Mr Sawdust mowing it.

But as for being so heavy she'd go through the floor of her hutch ... 'wheeee!' Olga gave another squeak of indignation. She'd show him. The very next time she was out in her run, where Noel would be able to see her properly, she'd show him.

As it happened, Olga's chance came sooner

than she'd expected. No sooner had she settled down and closed her eyes than the kitchen door opened once again and this time Karen Sawdust came out.

'Come on, Olga,' she said, as she opened the hutch door and lifted her out. 'It's time you had a bit of sunshine instead of lying in bed all day. It'll be autumn soon and you won't be able to. I should make the most of it.'

Karen Sawdust's remark was like fuel to Olga's fire. If she'd had any doubts about putting her plan into action before then they were now completely gone.

She could hardly wait for the moment when her run was turned over on to its face and she was able to scramble out of the built-up end and on to the open grass.

She gazed around. Luck was with her. Noel hadn't strayed far. He was sitting on a patch of stone near the pool washing himself. Graham was close by, doing something or other – goodness knew what. He was so slow it was hard to tell what he was up to sometimes. Even Fangio was busy catching flies in a corner of the lawn.

Olga waited until she heard the back door

close, then she took a deep breath, closed her eyes, heaved and braced herself for the fall.

After a moment or two, when nothing had happened, she opened her eyes again and found to her surprise that she was in exactly the same spot. She'd fully expected to be on the other side of her run at the very least. 'Perhaps,' she thought, 'I made a very soft landing. Guinea-pigs probably do on account of their silky fur.'

She gave a furtive look round the garden, but nothing had changed. Noel was still busy with his washing. He seemed to have found a par-ticularly difficult patch which demanded all his attention.

Taking a deep breath she tried again, only this time she kept her eyes open. It was most dis-appointing, but she had to admit, nothing, ab-solutely nothing, happened.

She tried a third time, then a fourth and a fifth. Still nothing. Panting after her exertions, she was trying to make up her mind whether to try once more or to have a rest for a while, when she felt someone or some*thing* close by staring at her.

'Are you all right?' asked Noel anxiously.

'Am I, huh, huh, hall right?' gasped Olga. 'Of course I'm , huh, huh, hall right. Why shouldn't I be? Wheeeeee! I've just been doing a bit of jogging, that's all.'

'Jogging!' Noel gave her a pitying stare. 'Jogging? You don't call that jogging, do you? You haven't even moved.'

'Wheeeeee! Yes, I have. You haven't been looking, that's your trouble. Too busy washing . . . wheeeeee!'

Olga was so incensed she rushed up and down her run, climbed up the side, took a wild bound and before she knew what was happening, felt herself flying through the air. Oblivious of the fact that in landing she'd knocked what was left of her breath right out of herself, she had another go. Now that she'd got the knack her delight knew no bounds. Or rather, it knew lots of bounds, for it felt as though her body had taken on wings.

Then, suddenly, she realized she was no longer alone. Noel let out a screech and disappeared as if his very life depended on it, and faces appeared above her run. Faces and voices. Mrs

Sawdust, Karen Sawdust, and several others she recognized as neighbours.

She felt herself being picked up.

'Olga! Olga! ... dear, oh dear! What's wrong?'

'I've never seen anything like it. Must be some kind of fit.'

'We'd better get her to the vet quickly.' Mrs Sawdust's voice took charge. 'You take her. Someone else find her box. I'll get the car out.'

Olga relaxed. Truth to tell, she felt like a

good lie down after all the rushing about. A drive in the car would be nice. It didn't matter to her if it was a wasted journey. Jogging took it out of you – especially if you weren't used to it. Especially . . . She pricked up her ears. One of the neighbours was talking.

'Perhaps the vet will put her to sleep. It'll be the kindest thing.'

'Put me to sleep? I do wish they'd make up their minds. First they want to take me to the vet. Now they want to put me to bed . . .' Gradually, the remark sank in and as it did so she felt a chill enter her stomach. It started somewhere in the middle and then spread all over her.

'There, there,' Karen Sawdust stroked her gently as she began to tremble. 'The vet'll know what to do for the best.'

'Wheeeeee!' Olga gave a shriek. It wasn't the vet's best that worried her, it was his worst. How could they not understand? How could she possibly begin to explain? If only Mr Sawdust was there – he might have known. 'Wheeeeeeee!' she collapsed into her travelling box in a terrible state.

Olga was hardly aware of the journey. Noises that would normally have made her look out with interest passed unheeded.

All she knew for certain was that worried faces kept peering down at her and that even her slightest movement or attempts at squeaking were taken as meaning the very worst.

In the end she gave up and just lay there.

'Hmmmm!' The vet turned her over and gave her stomach a few practised prods. Then he placed something cold and shiny on her chest and appeared to be listening to something.

'A fine time to be listening to the wireless,' thought Olga.

'Hmmm, yes . . . well,' the vet looked puzzled.

Olga lay back where she'd been put waiting for the worst.

'I can't find anything obviously wrong,' said the man.

Olga's hopes rose.

'And then again,' he rubbed his chin and Olga's hopes sank. 'She's probably had a narrow squeak.'

Olga gave a whimper. If her squeak had got narrow that must be a bad sign.

'I think,' he said at last, 'if you ask me, she could do with losing a bit of weight.'

Olga's hopes rose again. 'He knows,' she thought. 'He knows all about my jogging. He's probably going to tell them all about it.'

'Leave her with me,' said the vet briskly. 'I'll keep her under observation for a day or two. *And*,' he added sternly, 'I'll make sure she doesn't eat too much. I shall put her on a very strict diet. Leave her with me and I'll make a new guinea-pig of her.'

The vet was as good as his word. When Olga returned home almost a week later she was indeed a new guinea-pig. Even Noel had to look twice in order to make sure he was seeing aright. Her fur had a shiny glow to it; her eyes were fresh and sparkling; her movements quick and lithe; above all, she was in particularly good voice.

'I've been on a very long jog,' she announced as soon as she was settled into her house, 'and it's done me the world of good. Wheeeeeeee!

'If you're going to do something you may as well do it properly. Wheeeeee! Wheeeeeeee! You should try it sometime.

'I'm a new person. Wheeeèee! Wheeeeeeee! Wheeeeeeeeeee! I'll tell you all about if you like.'

But Noel wasn't having any. He looked up at her in disgust. 'I think,' he said, 'I much preferred the old one, thank you very much. At least it was quieter.'

And with that he disappeared into the house letting his pussy flap slam shut behind him.

'Wheeeeee!' said Olga. 'See how much I care.'

And she did a quick jog up and down, just to show she meant what she said.

Then she hesitated as she caught sight of her feeding bowl, full to the brim with luscious fresh oats.

Being fit was one thing, starving yourself was quite another matter. 'If I'm to be a new guinea-pig,' she thought, 'I may as well keep the best of the old.' And soon, save for a steady munching sound, all was quiet, and things were back to normal again. Olga had jogged for the very last time.

## CHAPTER EIGHT

# *Olga's Goodnight Story*

Soon after Olga gave up jogging there was a change in the weather. It suddenly grew much colder and Graham and Fangio began making hurried plans to hibernate for the winter, Fangio being torn between his usual hiding-place and his new house at the bottom of the garden, and Graham quite content with wherever the fancy took him at the time.

Even Noel trod more daintily as he came out to survey the estate before doing his daily rounds. No one ever knew quite where Noel went to on his rambles, but they seemed to follow a pattern which he varied from time to time − either to confuse his enemies or simply because he liked a change.

On this particular morning he seemed content to settle down near Olga's house while he watched the comings and goings.

It was while Olga was looking out on it all through her bedroom window that she noticed something very strange. When she put her nose close to the glass and breathed out it became all misty so that she could no longer see through it. She tried it several times and each time added to the first, so that in the end it was just like the special glass the Sawdust family had in their bathroom.

In the end, tiring of this and feeling rather thirsty after all the effort, she went into her dining-room to have a drink, only to discover that her bowl of water had a coating of ice over the top.

'Wheeeeee!' She gave a shrill squeak, which said, in effect, 'isn't it about time I was taken care of?'

The only effect it had on Noel was to make

him stare lazily in her direction as much as to say 'what's wrong now?'

'Wheeeeeeee!' said Olga. 'It's all very well for you. I expect you've had your breakfast, but I haven't. I'm hungry. Wheeeeeeee!'

'You'll be lucky,' grunted Noel. 'It's Sunday. They're all still in bed.'

'In that case,' said Olga, 'I shall give a very loud squeak. I shall squeak so loud it will go into the house, through your pussy flap, through the kitchen, then the hall, up the stairs and into the bedrooms, and it will wake them all up, so there!' And she took a deep, deep breath, just to show what she meant.

'Huh!' said Noel unsympathetically. 'Pigs might fly.'

It was a phrase he'd heard the Sawdust family use several evenings before and he'd been waiting to try it out on Olga, knowing it might upset her – for she hated being called a pig.

Olga paused, let out her breath and stared at Noel. 'Would you mind saying that again?' she demanded.

'Pigs might fly,' said Noel carelessly. 'That means it's never likely to happen.'

'Never likely to happen!' repeated Olga. '*Never likely to happen!*' She was so upset her imagination went soaring up into the clouds in an effort to think of something, anything, to wipe the superior look off Noel's face. As it did so her sharp ears caught the sound of an aeroplane high above in the sky. Suddenly an idea came into her mind.

'I'll have you know,' she said, 'that guinea-pigs are some of the best flyers in the world. Much better than birds. They can go much, much higher for a start.'

Noel's jaw dropped. He was used to Olga's extravagant claims and her tall stories, but this one threatened to be the tallest and most extravagant ever. Even Graham and Fangio stopped in their tracks as they passed by on their way down the garden.

Graham, who'd been about to say goodnight for the winter, looked most impressed.

'I never knew that,' he said. 'I hope it doesn't keep me awake. I don't suppose it will.'

Noel gave a disparaging snort. 'I've never seen a pig flying,' he said. 'Nor's anyone else.'

'Not *pigs*,' said Olga. 'They'd be much too heavy. *Guinea*-pigs.

'Guinea-pigs,' she went on, 'are as light as a feather. They're really all fur. The lightest, softest, downiest fur imaginable. Why, they're so light they have to be tied down sometimes to keep them on the ground. A puff of wind and they're away.

'Not like cat's fur. That's very thick and heavy. Now, *there's* something that couldn't possibly fly. Not in a million years.'

Noel's snort was almost as loud as Olga's squeak might have been had she ever made it.

'Show me one,' he said. 'Just show me one.'

Olga glanced up towards the sky again. She was only just in time, for the aeroplane was almost out of sight.

'There's one going over right now,' she said.

Her remark was greeted in silence.

'That's not a guinea-pig,' said Noel at last.

'It is,' said Olga firmly.

'How do you know it is?' said Noel. 'Prove it.'

'How do you know it *isn't*?' asked Olga, conscious of playing a trump card. 'You prove it isn't.'

For once Noel was stuck for an answer.

'If you can fly,' he said at last. 'Why don't

you? If you're so good at it, show us. You can't even jog, let alone fly.'

'Where are your wings?' piped up Fangio. 'I can't see them.'

'I keep them tucked away,' said Olga primly.

'Anyway,' she turned and stared pityingly at Noel, 'I couldn't possibly fly in here. I'd only bang my head on the roof. Besides, I'm a bit out of practice. That's the trouble with being stuck in a cage all day. It makes you stiff.'

'I wonder where it was going?' said Graham, who'd nearly ricked his neck trying to follow the progress of the plane.

'Probably somewhere warm for the winter,' said Fangio. 'That's what a lot of birds do.'

'Quite likely,' said Olga, glad that at least two members of her audience were on her side at last.

'Well, I still don't believe it,' said Noel. 'You might just as well say that was a tortoise,' he added, as a motor cycle roared past outside.

'If you think *that* you'll think anything,' said Olga. 'Besides, it was going much too fast.'

'The thing is,' she continued, 'it all began many, many years ago, long before any of us were born, in the days when guinea-pigs lived in caves.

'That's why we're called "cavies", you know – because we once lived in caves.'

'That's true,' said Graham. 'I've heard that.'

'I live in a garage,' said Fangio, 'but I'm not called a "garages".'

Olga ignored the interruption. It really wasn't worth replying to.

'Some of you,' she went on, looking pointed-ly towards Noel, '*may* be able to picture what it must have been like all those years ago when they first saw daylight. Picture living in a big cave all your life, in the dark, and then suddenly one day finding the way out into the daylight.

'They were so excited they jumped for joy and to their astonishment they found them-selves floating. And because they were so light and because they were already high up, for the cave was at the top of a high mountain, they floated way, way up into the sky.

'That's how they ended up in so many dif-ferent parts of the world. I expect my ancestors landed in the pet shop down the road and that's how I came to be here.'

Olga settled back, well pleased with her tale.
Once she'd got going it had all fallen into place
very nicely indeed.

As she did so another aeroplane, going very fast this time, and much lower, shot by. Fortunately, it was on the other side of the house and out of sight.

'There goes another one,' she said. 'It sounded as if it was in a hurry to get somewhere. I expect it's going off to do a good deed. Guinea-pigs are always doing good deeds somewhere or ot' ~r you know.'

Noel made a choking sound.

'Is something the matter?' asked Olga innocently.

Noel glared up at the sky where a distant drone and a long vapour trail showed where yet another plane was passing overhead. 'You'll be saying next they blow steam out of their noses like those dragons you told us about once.'

'I'm very glad you mentioned that,' said Olga. 'They're what's known as guinea-pig trails. Every time you see them it means there's a guinea-pig going somewhere.

'If you hadn't mentioned it I might have forgotten to tell you. You see, I may not be able to fly myself any more, but that's one thing I *can* still do – make trails.'

And so saying, she hurried into her bedroom, took up her position behind the window, drew in the deepest breath she could manage, and blew out as hard as she could.

'Well I never!' said Graham, as Olga's window went misty. 'Would you believe it?'

'*I* wouldn't have,' said Fangio. 'But I do now.'

Olga hurried out into her dining-room. 'How about you?' she called to Noel. 'Do you believe it now?' But Noel was already disappearing over the fence. He'd seen a squirrel and that was much more interesting.

'Goodnight,' said Graham. 'I shall sleep well after that.'

'Hear! Hear!' agreed Fangio. 'See you next spring.'

'Goodnight,' said Olga. She gazed after the other two as they went on their way. 'If you have any trouble getting to sleep, try counting guinea-pigs,' she called. 'They go over every day. I think I can hear another one coming now.'

'Oh, we shan't,' came a sleepy voice, barely

recognizable as Graham's. 'Not after that. Stories make you sleepy.'

With that remark Olga agreed wholeheartedly. In fact, she went straight back into her bedroom and closed her eyes. Within moments she was fast asleep. But not for the winter, only until it was time for Sunday morning breakfast and another day.